# CAPTAIN UNDERPANTS AND THE WRATH OF THE WICKED WEDGIE WOMAN

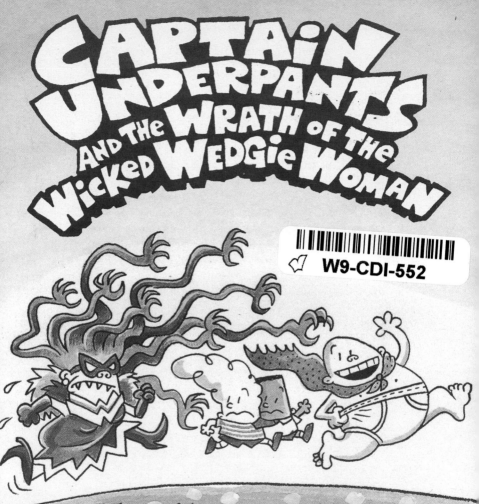

The Fifth Epic Novel by

# DAV PILKEY

SCHOLASTIC INC.
New York  Toronto  London  Auckland  Sydney
Mexico City  New Delhi  Hong Kong  Buenos Aires

*Special thanks to:*
*Devin, Tanner, and Adam Long*

This book is being published simultaneously in hardcover by the Blue Sky Press.

ISBN 978-0-439-05000-5 (Trade) / ISBN 978-0-545-38572-5 (BC)

The quote by Albert Einstein is from an interview in the October 26, 1929,
issue of *The Saturday Evening Post*.

Be sure to check out Dav Pilkey's Extra-Crunchy Web Site O' Fun at
www.pilkey.com.

10 9 8 7 6 5 4 3 2 1                           11 12 13 14 15 16/0

Printed in the United States of America          40

First Scholastic paperback printing, September 2001

"Imagination is more important
than knowledge."
—Albert Einstein

# CHAPTERS

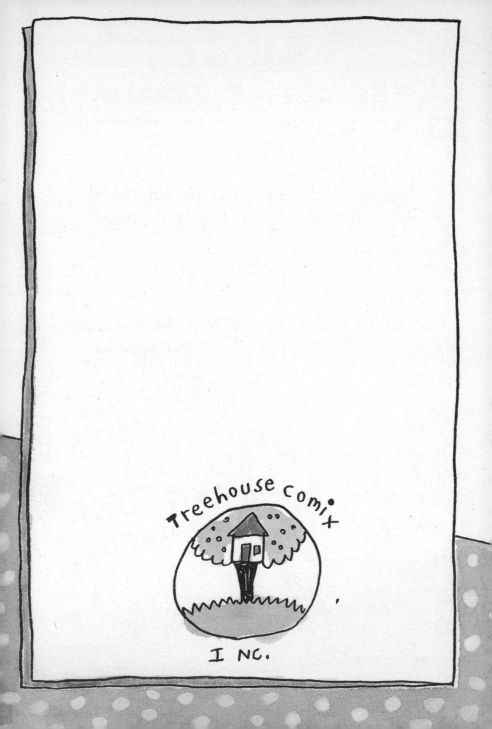

# CHAPTER 1
## GEORGE AND HAROLD

This is George Beard and Harold Hutchins.
George is the kid on the left with the tie
and the flat-top. Harold is the one on the
right with the T-shirt and the bad haircut.
Remember that now.

At most schools, the teachers try to emphasize "the three **R**s" (**R**eading, '**R**iting, and '**R**ithmetic). But George and Harold's teacher Ms. Ribble was more concerned with enforcing what she called "the three **S**s" (**S**it down, **S**hut your pie holes, and **S**TOP DRIVING ME CRAZY!)

While this was unfortunate for all of her students, it was especially bad for

George and Harold, because they were very imaginative boys.

You see, imagination was not really encouraged at George and Harold's school— in fact, it was discouraged. "Imagination" would only get you a one-way ticket to the principal's office.

This was sad for George and Harold, because they didn't get straight As, they weren't sports stars, and they could barely walk down the hallway without getting into trouble. . . .

PLEASE GO
PEE-PEE
ON YOUR
SOCKS FOR
WARMTH

I LOL

. . . See what I mean?!!?

But George and Harold had one thing
that most of the other folks at Jerome
Horwitz Elementary School didn't have:
*Imagination*. They were *full* of it! And one
day they would use that imagination to save
the entire human race from being over-
thrown by a crazed woman with even crazier
super powers.

But before I can tell you that story, I have
to tell you *this* story. . . .

# CHAPTER 2
# MS. RIBBLE'S BIG NEWS

One fine day, George and Harold's homeroom teacher, Ms. Ribble, entered the classroom looking a bit meaner than usual.

"Alright, settle down!" shouted Ms. Ribble. "I have some bad news: I'm retiring."

"Hooray!" cried the children.

*"Not today!"* snapped Ms. Ribble. "At the end of the school year!"

"Aww, *maaaan,*" moaned the children.

"But the staff is throwing a retirement party for me today . . ." said Ms. Ribble.

"Hooray!" cried the children.

". . . during recess," said Ms. Ribble.

"Aww, *maaaan,*" moaned the children.

"There will be lots of free ice cream!"
said Ms. Ribble.

"Hooray!" cried the children.

"My favorite flavor: *chunky tofu!*" said
Ms. Ribble.

"Aww, *maaaan*," moaned the children.

"But first," said Ms. Ribble, "it's time for
something fun!"

"Hooray!" cried the children.

"You all get to make 'Happy Retirement'
cards for me!" said Ms. Ribble.

"Aww, *maaaan*," moaned the children.

16

# CHAPTER 3

# WHEN YOU CARE ENOUGH TO SEND THE VERY BEST

Ms. Ribble went around the classroom handing out envelopes, sheets of construction paper, and butterfly stencils to all of the children. Then she wrote a poem on the chalkboard.

"Alright, take out your crayons," said Ms. Ribble harshly. "I want you to use stencils to make a yellow butterfly on the front of your cards. When you're done, copy this poem on the inside."

Roses are Red,
Violets are Blue.
You are Retiring
And We'll Miss You.
Signed,
Your Name Here

"Can we make up our own poems?" asked Melvin Sneedly.

"*No!*" snapped Ms. Ribble.

"Do we have to use stencils?" asked Aaron Mancini.

"YES!" yelled Ms. Ribble.

"Can we make our butterflies purple?" asked Stephanie Yarkoff.

*"NO!"* screamed Ms. Ribble. "Butterflies are yellow! Everyone knows that!"

While the rest of the class worked on their cards, George and Harold had a better idea.

"Let's make Ms. Ribble a comic book instead!" said George.

"Yeah!" said Harold. "We can make it all about her. It'll be cool!"

So that's just what they did.

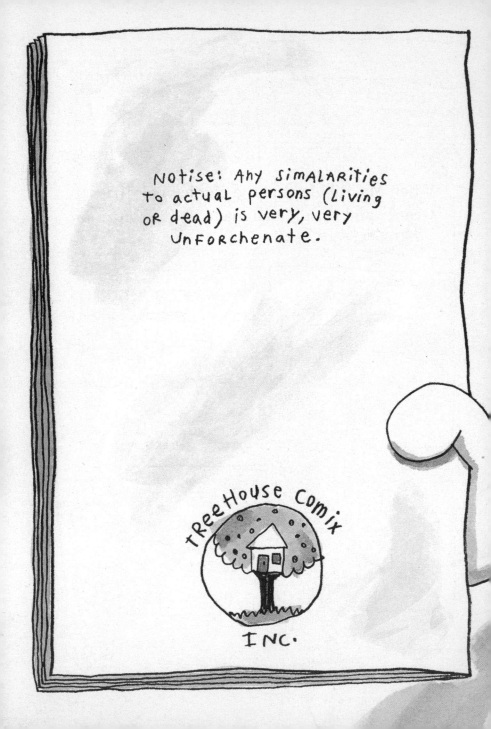

NOTISE: Any SIMALARITIES
to actual persons (Living
or dead) is very, very
UnForchenate.

TReeHouse Comix
INC.

## CHAPTER 5

# THE WRATH OF
# MS. RIBBLE

When Ms. Ribble read the comic book that
George and Harold had made, she was furious.

"Boys!" she yelled. "You've just earned
yourselves a one-way ticket to the principal's
office!"

"But all we did was use our imaginations!"
said George.

"You're not allowed to do that in this
school!" snapped Ms. Ribble. "Didn't you read
chapter 1?"

George and Harold gathered their things, and soon they were sitting in the office outside Mr. Krupp's door.

"Mr. Krupp is on the phone," said the school secretary, Miss Anthrope. "Why don't you boys make yourselves useful and copy the 'Friday Memo' for me! You can pass them out to all the classrooms for me while I go to lunch."

"Aww, *maaaan!*" said George.

*"Quit your whining, buster!"* shouted Miss Anthrope. "I want this done by the time I get back, or you'll *both* be sorry!" Miss Anthrope grabbed her coat and stomped out the door.

## Jerome Horwitz Elementary School
# Friday Memo

### Next Week's News:

**Monday:** BAND PRACTICE CANCELLED. No practice today due to asbestos removal in gymnasium.

**Tuesday:** SCHOOL SPIRIT DAY! Show your school spirit by wearing the school colors (gray and dark gray).

**Wednesday:** CHEERLEADER TRYOUTS TODAY: Anyone wishing to join the cheerleading squad must do all of the following:
1) Meet in the gym after school.
2) Have the school cheer memorized.
3) Don't forget to wear gym shoes.

**Thursday:** FOOTBALL PRACTICE RE-SCHEDULED. All football players report to soccer field for early practice— *today only*. Pep Rally @ 3:15 in the gym.

**Friday:** YEARBOOK PHOTOS TAKEN TODAY: (Please dress appropriately!) Anyone caught making "funny" faces will receive a detention.

George and Harold looked at the "Friday Memo." It was a weekly newsletter that told all about the events of the upcoming week.

"Hey," said George. "Miss Anthrope's computer is still on. Y'wanna make a few changes to this newsletter?"

"Why not?" said Harold.

33

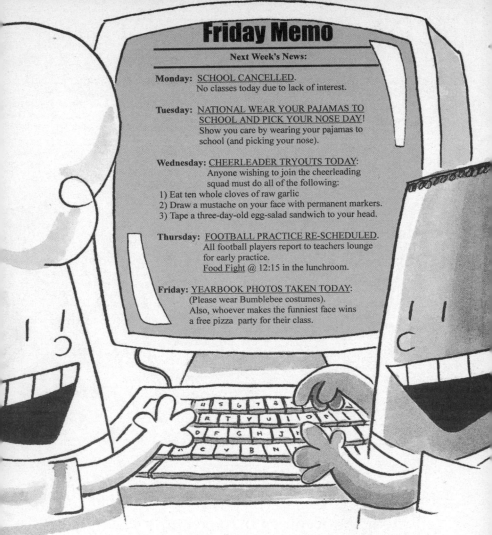

**Friday Memo**

**Next Week's News:**

**Monday:** <u>SCHOOL CANCELLED</u>.
No classes today due to lack of interest.

**Tuesday:** <u>NATIONAL WEAR YOUR PAJAMAS TO SCHOOL AND PICK YOUR NOSE DAY</u>!
Show you care by wearing your pajamas to school (and picking your nose).

**Wednesday:** <u>CHEERLEADER TRYOUTS TODAY</u>:
Anyone wishing to join the cheerleading squad must do all of the following:
1) Eat ten whole cloves of raw garlic
2) Draw a mustache on your face with permanent markers.
3) Tape a three-day-old egg-salad sandwich to your head.

**Thursday:** <u>FOOTBALL PRACTICE RE-SCHEDULED</u>.
All football players report to teachers lounge for early practice.
<u>Food Fight</u> @ 12:15 in the lunchroom.

**Friday:** <u>YEARBOOK PHOTOS TAKEN TODAY</u>:
(Please wear Bumblebee costumes).
Also, whoever makes the funniest face wins a free pizza party for their class.

So George and Harold typed up their own version of the "Jerome Horwitz Elementary School Friday Memo." Then they ran off copies for all the students in the school.

## CHAPTER 6
# THE RETIREMENT CARD

George and Harold were gathering their
new-and-improved "Friday Memo" copies
into small piles when Principal Krupp came
into the office.

*"Hey!"* Mr. Krupp shouted. "What are you
two troublemakers doing in here?"

"Miss Anthrope told us to pass the 'Friday
Memo' out to all the classrooms," said
George innocently.

"Well, make it snappy!" yelled Principal
Krupp.

Suddenly, Harold got a sneaky idea. He
took out the blank piece of construction
paper that Ms. Ribble had given him earlier.

"Hey, Mr. Krupp," said Harold, "will you
sign this retirement card for our teacher?"

Mr. Krupp grabbed the card from Harold
and eyed it suspiciously.

"This card is *blank*!" Mr. Krupp growled.

"I know," said Harold. "Our class is going
to decorate it later. We wanted you to be the
first to sign it."

"Well, alright then," said Mr. Krupp.
He opened the card and quickly scribbled

*Signed, Mr. Krupp*

on the inside. Then he stormed out of
the office.

"What are you gonna do with that?"
asked George.

"You'll see," said Harold, smiling.

# CHAPTER 7
# REVERSE PSYCHOLOGY

George and Harold passed out the "Friday Memo" and made it back to their classroom just in time for Ms. Ribble's retirement party. George quickly changed the letters around on the sign outside the door, while Harold wrote a special greeting on Mr. Krupp's card and stuffed it into the envelope.

HAVE A BLISSFULLY GRAND RETIREMENT MS. RIBBLE

"*HEY, BUBS!*" shouted Mr. Krupp as he stormed down the hall. "What do you kids think you're doing?"

"We're going to Ms. Ribble's retirement party," said George.

"That's what *YOU* think, smart guy!" said Mr. Krupp. "Ms. Ribble showed me that comic book you boys made about her. And now I catch you changing the letters around on another sign! You boys aren't going to any party . . . you're going STRAIGHT to the detention room!"

"Well *fine*," said Harold. "Then we're not gonna give Ms. Ribble the card our class made for her!"

Mr. Krupp quickly swiped the card out of Harold's hand.

"A-HA!" he shouted. "I'm going to make SURE she gets this card! I'm going to give it to her *MYSELF*!"

"Aww, *maaaan!*" said Harold.

George and Harold walked down the hallway toward the detention room.

"Wow," said George. "That was pretty cool
how you got Mr. Krupp to deliver that phony
card for you."

"Yep," said Harold. "I used *reverse
psychology* on him!"

"I've gotta try that sometime," said George.
"By the way, what did you write on that card?"

"You'll see," said Harold, smiling.

# CHAPTER 8
# THE PARTY

Ms. Ribble's retirement party started off bad, and just got worse. First, Ms. Ribble forced the class to sing a corny song to her. By the time she was done yelling at the boys for singing off-key, the chunky tofu ice cream was melted.

Everybody had to eat it anyway.

Then the children handed in their "Happy Retirement" cards. Ms. Ribble ripped several of the cards up because some of the children had mistakenly drawn polka-dots on their butterflies. One unfortunate boy had also drawn a happy "smiling" sunshine on his card, and he had to stand in the corner.

Finally, Mr. Krupp stepped forward and handed Ms. Ribble the card he had snatched from Harold's hand.

"I went to a lot of trouble to get this for you," Mr. Krupp said gallantly.

Ms. Ribble tore the envelope open, and read the card out loud:

"You're One *Hot Mama*!" said Ms. Ribble, with a shocked look on her face.

"Eeeeeeeeew!" cried the children.

She opened the card and read the inside.
"Will you marry me? Signed, Mr. Krupp."

"Eeeeeeeeeeeeeeeeeeeeeeeeeeeeewww!"
cried the children. The teachers gasped. Then
the room grew silent. Ms. Ribble glared over
at Mr. Krupp, who had turned bright red and
began sweating profusely.

He tried to speak. He tried to tell her it
was all a big mistake. He tried to say SOME-
THING . . . but all that came out was "B-b-
bubba bobba hobhobba-hobba Wah-wah."

"Er, ummm, *congratulations*," said Mr. Meaner, as he patted Mr. Krupp's sweaty, shivering shoulder.

"Yes! CONGRATULATIONS!" shouted Miss Anthrope. "This will be the best wedding in the whole world! We can have it here at the school . . . a week from Saturday! I'll plan everything! You lovebirds don't have to worry about a thing!"

"Er-uh, . . . great . . . thanks," said Ms.
Ribble, still looking quite angry and confused.

"B-b-bubba bobba hob-hobba-hobba
Wah-wah," said Mr. Krupp.

# CHAPTER 9
# FREAKY WEEKY

The following week at Jerome Horwitz Elementary School was definitely one of the weirdest ones they'd had in a while. For example: None of the kids showed up for school on Monday. But Mr. Krupp didn't even seem to notice.

"Hey, where is everybody today?" asked Mr. Rected.

"B-b-bubba bobba hob-hobba-hobba Wah-wah," said Mr. Krupp.

On Tuesday everybody did show up . . . in their pajamas!

"Why is everybody picking their noses?" asked Miss Fitt.

"B-b-bubba bobba hob-hobba-hobba Wah-wah," said Mr. Krupp.

On Wednesday for some strange reason,
the whole school smelled like garlic and
rotten egg-salad sandwiches (especially some
of the girls).

"Boy," said Ms. Guided, "the styles today
sure are getting bizarre."

"B-b-bubba bobba hob-hobba-hobba
Wah-wah," said Mr. Krupp.

Thursday was, without a doubt, a complete and total disaster.

*"There's a food fight in the lunchroom!"* shouted Mr. Rustworthy. "And the football team is destroying the teacher's lounge!"

"B-b-bubba bobba hob-hobba-hobba Wah-wah," said Mr. Krupp.

Now, *nobody* was sure what happened on Friday. Apparently there was a mix-up with the dress code and the yearbook photos.

"Our school pictures are ruined!" shouted Ms. Dayken.

"B-b-bubba bobba hob-hobba-hobba Wah-wah," said Mr. Krupp.

Yes, it was a freaky week, alright. But the big wedding was only a day away . . . and things were about to get REALLY freaky!

# CHAPTER 10

# THE BIG WEDDING

It was Saturday, the day of the big wedding. Miss Anthrope, true to her word, had taken care of everything. In just one week, she had transformed the gymnasium into a beautiful wedding hall, complete with food, decorations, and even a six-foot-tall ice sculpture.

All of the children were dressed in their finest clothes. (Harold even wore a tie!)

"Man," said George, "I can't believe we have to go to school on *SATURDAY*!"

"I know," said Harold. "Why couldn't they have had this wedding during Monday's math test?"

Soon the organist began to play. The rabbi walked down the aisle. He approached George and Harold and stopped to talk to the boys.

"I've heard a lot about you two," said the rabbi, "and I don't want you boys playing any of your tricks today."

"Silly Rabbi," said George, "tricks are for kids!"

Believe it or not, George and Harold had not planned any pranks for the big wedding. They had no "Joy Buzzers" up their sleeves . . . no squirting flowers in their lapels . . . and no whoopee cushions on their chairs. They were on their best behavior. Nothing could go wrong today!

In no time at all, Ms. Ribble and Mr. Krupp were standing in front of the rabbi, looking quite ill. The rabbi asked Mr. Krupp if he would take Ms. Ribble to be his lawfully wedded wife.

"B-b-bubba bobba hob-hobba-hobba Wah-wah," said Mr. Krupp.

Then the rabbi asked Ms. Ribble if she would take Mr. Krupp to be her husband.

There was a long silence. Everyone leaned forward. Ms. Ribble looked nervously from side to side.

Suddenly, she shouted out at the top of her lungs, *"NOOOOOOOOOOOOOOOOO!"*

Ms. Ribble turned to Mr. Krupp and
jabbed her finger into his shoulder. "Listen,
Krupp," she said. "I *can't* marry you."

"Hooray!—er, I mean—*aww, that's too
bad*!" said Mr. Krupp.

"You're a mean, cruel, and vicious man,"
said Ms. Ribble, "and I respect that. It's
just . . . it's just . . ."

"Just what?" asked Mr. Krupp.

"It's just your *nose*!" said Ms. Ribble.
"You've got the most *ridiculous* nose—
I've never seen anything quite like it! I just
couldn't marry somebody with such a
silly nose."

Mr. Krupp got angry. "Well *fine*!" he shouted. "I didn't want to marry you anyway! It was all George and Harold's fault. They *tricked* us!"

Suddenly, everybody in the gymnasium turned and looked at George and Harold.

"Time to go," said George.

# CHAPTER 11
# THE REFRESHMENTS

As George and Harold turned to leave the gymnasium, they heard the loud thumps of cleated wedding boots clomping down the aisle toward them.

"I'M GONNA GRIND THOSE KIDS INTO HEAD CHEESE!" screamed Ms. Ribble as she lunged for the two boys.

George and Harold screamed and ran to the back of the room near the refreshments. There they hid behind two large wooden pillars.

Ms. Ribble approached the pillars and grasped them with her mighty hands. With a horrible roar, she pushed the right pillar over. It landed on the back of the luncheon table, causing the front of the table to flip high into the air. Unfortunately, this sent all of the food flying into the crowd.

CRASH

The creamy candied carrots clobbered
the kindergarteners. The fatty fried fish
fritters flipped onto the first graders. The
sweet-n-sour spaghetti squash splattered the
second graders.

Three thousand thawing thimbleberries thudded the third graders. Five hundred frosted fudgy fruitcakes flogged the fourth graders. And fifty-five fistfuls of fancy French-fried frankfurters flattened the fifth graders.

By now you're probably worried that the wedding guests had nothing to drink with their lovely appetizers. Well, rest assured, the second pillar took care of that. Ms. Ribble pushed the left pillar into the fresh fruit display, causing it to topple over, sending

two large watermelons crashing down into
two oversized punch bowls. This created two
enormous splashes of tropical fruit-flavored
punch, which rained down upon the wedding
guests like a torrential downpour.

Now, no wedding is complete without a
wedding cake. And when Ms. Ribble kicked
the ice sculpture over, the resulting crash
sent the beautiful double-deckered cake
flipping high into the air, right over Ms.
Ribble's head.

"I'VE GOT YOU NOW!"
screamed Ms. Ribble, as
she grabbed George
and Harold by
their neckties.

# SPLAT

George and Harold undid their ties and ran out of the gymnasium screaming.

"Man," cried Harold. "I thought we were dead meat!"

"That's what we get for going to school on Saturday!" said George.

# CHAPTER 12
# RIBBLE'S REVENGE

As you might imagine, George and Harold were nervous about going back to class on Monday. But for some strange reason, Ms. Ribble seemed happy to see them.

"Good morning, boys," Ms. Ribble chirped with a giant, evil, toothy grin. "Come here . . . I've got something to show you!"

"Uh, oh," said George. "She's smiling— that *can't* be a good sign!"

George and Harold cautiously approached Ms. Ribble's desk.

"I took the liberty of adjusting your grades last weekend," said Ms. Ribble. "You'll be happy to know that all your grades have just dropped from Bs and Cs to *Fs and Gs.*"

"Oh, *NO!*" George gasped. "Not *Fs and Gs!* . . . Hey, what's a *G*?"

"It's the only grade *lower* than an *F*!" said Ms. Ribble.

"There's no such grade as a *G*," said Harold.

"There is now, bub!" said Ms. Ribble. "Looks like you're both going to *FLUNK* the FOURTH GRADE!!! Won't that be fun?"

"No way," said George. *"That's not fair!"*

"Life ain't fair," said Ms. Ribble. "Get used to it!"

# CHAPTER 13
# A BAD IDEA

That afternoon, George and Harold sat in their tree house feeling sorry for themselves.

"She can't get away with that," said George. "We've got to tell somebody about this."

"Nobody's going to believe us," said Harold.

"Well, there is *one* thing we can do," said George. He opened the drawer to their drawing table and searched through the pennies, paper clips, dried spitballs, and rubber bands. Then he pulled out a dusty plastic ring with some gum stuck on it. It was the 3-D Hypno-Ring.

"Oh, no!" said Harold. "I thought we threw that thing away!"

"We just threw the instructions away," said George. "But I remember how it works."

"Do you *remember* what happened the LAST TIME WE USED IT?" asked Harold.

"Yeah," said George. "But we were fooling around last time. This time we'll be serious. We won't make any mistakes! All we have to do is hypnotize her into changing our grades back to normal. That's all!"

"I don't know . . ." said Harold. "It sounds like a bad idea to me!"

"Worse than *FLUNKING* the fourth grade?" asked George.

"Good point," said Harold.

# CHAPTER 14

# THE RETURN OF THE 3-D HYPNO-RING

The next day at school, George and Harold stayed behind while the rest of the class went outside for recess.

"What are you punks still doing here?" asked Ms. Ribble.

"Ummmm," said George nervously. "Er, we wanted to show you this really cool ring."

"Yeah," said Harold. "If you look closely at it, you can see a funny picture."

"Well, hold it still," said Ms. Ribble, as she stared at the ring intently.

"I have to move it back and forth," said George, "or you won't be able to see the picture."

Ms. Ribble's eyes followed the ring back and forth . . . back and forth . . . back and forth . . . back and forth. . . .

"You are getting sleepy," said George.

"Veeery sleepy," said Harold.

Ms. Ribble yawned. Her eyes began to droop.

"I'mmssooosleeeeepyyy," she said, as she slowly closed her eyes.

"In a moment," said George, "I will snap my fingers. Then you will be hypnotized."

"Sssssooooosssslllleeeeeeeeepyyyyyyy," mumbled Ms. Ribble.

*SNAP!*

"Now," said Harold, "you must listen very . . ."

## CHAPTER 14½

# WE INTERRUPT THIS CHAPTER TO BRING YOU THIS IMPORTANT MESSAGE:

"Hello, This is Chim-Chim Diaperbrains . . . er, I mean, this is Ingrid Ashley reporting for Eyewitness News. We have a late-breaking story about a tragic incident that is now occurring in the Pacific Northwest.

"Police have just closed down the Li'l Wiseguy Novelty Company in Walla-Walla, Washington. Apparently, this company has been selling very dangerous 'Hypno-Rings.' We now take you live, via satellite to our reporter, Booger Stinkersquirt, er, I mean, Larry Zarrow, with the latest developments."

"Thanks, Chim-Chim," said Larry. "Reports have poured in from all across the country concerning children who have used the '3-D Hypno-Ring' on their friends and family with disastrous results. But the most shocking revelation is the effect that the rings seem to have on *women*.

"Apparently, whenever the ring is used to hypnotize a woman, a mental blunder occurs, causing the woman to do the OPPO-SITE of what she is being hypnotized to do.

"Doctors don't know why the ring causes women to have an OPPOSITE reaction, but they are very concerned. If you or someone you love has purchased a '3-D Hypno-Ring,' throw it away at once. And whatever you do, PLEASE DON'T USE IT ON A WOMAN!"

# CHAPTER 14³/₄

# WE NOW RETURN TO OUR REGULARLY SCHEDULED CHAPTER (ALREADY IN PROGRESS...)

". . . and when we snap our fingers," George continued, "you will change our grades back to normal."

"Yeah," said Harold. "And you won't do anything crazy, like turn into *Wedgie Woman*."

"And you won't try to destroy Captain Underpants," said George, "or take over the world, either."

"Right!" said Harold. "You'll just change our grades, and that's it!"

George and Harold looked nervously at each other.

"Well," said George, "I think that covers everything."

"Yep," said Harold. "We shouldn't have any more problems from Ms. Ribble."

So the boys snapped their fingers.

*SNAP!*

# CHAPTER 15
# BAD HAIR NIGHT

That night, Harold and George camped out in George's tree house.

"I have to drive your mother to work early tomorrow morning," said George's dad. "So you boys are responsible for getting yourselves to school on time."

"O.K., Pop," said George.

"We'll be there bright and early, Mr. Beard," said Harold.

It had been a tough day for George and Harold, and now it was time to relax. George rolled out the sleeping bags, while Harold unpacked a box of chocolate donuts, four cans of orange cream soda, and a big bowl of Bar-B-Q potato chips. Believe it or not, there was even a cool Japanese monster movie playing on TV.

"You know," said George, "life doesn't get any better than this!"

"Yep," said Harold. "But do you think the Hypno-Ring actually worked on Ms. Ribble? She looked a little weird when she came out of her trance."

"Aaah, she was probably just sleepy," said George. "Teachers have very stressful jobs, you know."

"I wonder why?" said Harold.

After the movie, George and Harold brushed the crumbs out of their sleeping bags and got ready for bed.

"Let's sleep in our school clothes tonight," said George. "That way we won't have to wake up early to get dressed."

"Good idea," said Harold.

So George turned out the light, and soon the two boys were drifting off to sleep. After a few minutes, Harold sat up quickly and looked around.

"Hey!" he whispered. "What's that noise?"

"I didn't hear anything," said George.

They listened closely.

"Shhh!" said Harold. "There it is again!"

George heard it this time. He reached over and opened the tree house door a crack. All they could hear was the sound of crickets chirping in the night. George opened the door wider, and the boys peeked down.

"AAAUUGH!" roared an evil-looking woman dressed in tight purple vinyl and a mangy-looking fake-fur boa.

George and Harold screamed in horror!

The snarling woman climbed from the ladder into the tree house. George and Harold recognized her immediately in the moonlight.

86

*"Ms. Ribble,"* George gasped. "What a lovely, uh, *outfit* you have on."

"Who's Ms. Ribble?" the angry lady growled. "My name is *Wedgie Woman*!!!"

George and Harold looked at each other and swallowed hard.

"I understand that you boys have information about Captain Underpants," said Wedgie Woman.

"What makes you say that?" asked Harold.

"I've read your comic books," said the evil villain. "You boys know his strengths, his weaknesses, and I'll bet you even know his SECRET IDENTITY!"

"No way!" said George. "Captain Underpants isn't real. . . . He-he's just a cartoon!"

"We'll see about that," Wedgie Woman scoffed.

Wedgie Woman reached out and grasped
George and Harold's arms.

"What do we do now?" cried Harold.

"We can take 'er," said George. "It's not
like she has super powers or anything!"

# CHAPTER 16

# WHO'S AFRAID OF THE BIG BAD BEEHIVE?

The struggle that followed may someday be remembered as the single most unlucky thing that ever happened in the history of the world.

First, George pulled his arm out of Wedgie Woman's grasp. Then Harold squirmed away, too. When Wedgie Woman lunged after them, George crouched down into a ball behind Wedgie Woman's feet. All it took was a simple nudge from Harold to send the ferocious female toppling over backward . . .

EXTRA STRENGTH SUPER POWER JUICE

. . . right into the wall. KLUNK! The book-shelf above Wedgie Woman's head shook vio-lently, causing a strange-looking juice carton to topple over. Suddenly, a stream of glowing green juice poured out of the carton, directly into the tightly woven beehive of hair atop Wedgie Woman's head.

"NOOO!" yelled Harold as he grabbed the juice carton. "This is the juice we got from that spaceship back in our third book!"

"You mean the one with the annoyingly long title?" asked George.

"Yeah!" said Harold. "This is EXTRA-STRENGTH SUPER POWER JUICE! And a whole bunch of it got in her hair!"

"Don't worry," said George. "None of it got in her mouth. What's the worst thing that could happen? Her *hairstyle* would have super powers?"

"Well," said Harold, "I guess you're right. That *is* pretty stupid . . . even for one of *our* stories!"

"It's pretty funny, though," said George.

Suddenly, two coiled arms of twisting hair shot out of Wedgie Woman's head and grabbed George and Harold by the back of their underwear, yanking them high into the air.

"You know," said George, "this isn't as funny as I thought it would be."

## CHAPTER 17
# ALL TIED UP

Wedgie Woman brought George and Harold back to her house and tied the boys tightly to two chairs.

"Tell me the secret identity of Captain Underpants!" screamed Wedgie Woman.

"No way!" said George.

"Hmmmm," said Wedgie Woman. "You want to do this the hard way? *No problem!*"

Wedgie Woman's hair began uncoiling itself. Several twisted locks of hair stretched out into the living room and started taking apart the television, the computer, and a Thighmaster®.

Other tangled coils reached into the kitchen and began dismantling the dishwasher, the toaster oven, and a Ronco™ Food Dehydrator.

"What are you doing?" asked Harold.

"If you want to make robots," said Wedgie Woman, "you gotta break a few small appliances!"

MEANEST
**TEACHER**
OF THE
YEAR AWARD

George and Harold watched impatiently while Wedgie Woman's hair assembled thousands of assorted screws, bolts, wires, gears, cathode tubes, and computer chips. Soon, two small robots began taking shape.

"I didn't know Ms. Ribble was smart enough to make robots," said Harold.

"Me, neither," said George. "I think some of that EXTRA-STRENGTH SUPER POWER JUICE must have soaked into her *brain*!"

The next morning, Wedgie Woman completed her robots, which she named "Robo-George" and "The Harold 2000."

"You know," said Harold, "something about those robots seems a little *familiar*!"

"Yeah," said George. "They kinda look like us . . . only not as dashingly handsome."

Wedgie Woman opened the robots' chest plates and inserted a can of spray starch into each one. Then she sealed the chest plates, patted each robot on the head, and sent them both off to school. "Captain Underpants doesn't stand a chance now!" Wedgie Woman laughed.

"Wait a minute," said Harold. "How are those two robots going to stop Captain Underpants?"

"All they have to do is wait and listen," said Wedgie Woman. "And as soon as they hear the words 'Tra-La-Laaaaa!', *it'll all be over*!"

# CHAPTER 18

# ROBO-GEORGE AND THE HAROLD 2000

"Uh, attention boys and girls," said Mr. Krupp to the fourth graders. "Your teacher, Ms. Ribble, didn't come to school today."

"Hooray!" shouted the children.

*"Settle down!"* Mr. Krupp shouted. "You're still going to have all your classes!"

"Aww, *maaaan!*" moaned the children.

"But you're going to have a substitute teacher," said Mr. Krupp.

"Hooray!" shouted the children.

"And it's going to be *me!*" said Mr. Krupp.

"Aww, *maaaan!*" moaned the children.

The whole day was pretty much like a normal day, except for one thing: Mr. Krupp couldn't understand why George and Harold were so well behaved.

They didn't make funny noises during science class, they didn't stick crayons up their noses during art class, and they didn't draw comic books during math class. In fact, they even walked past a sign without changing the letters around. Mr. Krupp was stunned.

"Alright, you two!" Mr. Krupp shouted. "I know you're up to something. . . . You better stop being so good, or you're gonna be in *BIG TROUBLE*!"

TODAY'S LUNCH

GENETICALLY MODIFIED MEAT FLAVORED BEEF

WITH EXTRA BOVINE GROWTH HORMONES

But Robo-George and the Harold 2000
kept right on behaving. The only time they
did something even remotely wrong was during recess. Everybody was playing kickball,
and when it was the Harold 2000's turn to
kick the ball, he kicked it pretty darn hard.

*KA-BOINGGG!*

The kickball tore right through the top of page 101 and out the other side as it sailed toward the outer regions of Earth's atmosphere. Soon it broke free of our planet's gravitational pull and began heading straight toward the planet Uranus.

"A-HA!" shouted Mr. Krupp, as he pulled out the official school rulebook and read Rule #411 out loud: *It is against the rules to kick school property into outer space!* You're in trouble now, bub!"

But the Harold 2000 ignored Mr. Krupp and began running around the bases.

"Hey! I'm talking to you, Hutchins!" Mr. Krupp shouted. He pointed at the Harold 2000 and snapped his fingers.

*SNAP!*

Suddenly, Mr. Krupp began to change. A silly-looking smile stretched across his face, and he stood before the fourth graders looking quite heroic. Quickly, he turned and ran back into the school.

# CHAPTER 19
# TRA-LA-LUUUNATICS

Several minutes later, Captain Underpants flew out of Mr. Krupp's office window. As the hero zipped across the sky, he let out a triumphant "Tra-La-Laaaaa!"

When Robo-George and the Harold 2000 heard the words "Tra-La-Laaaaa!", they immediately stopped playing kickball. Suddenly, their arms began to extend and their legs stretched toward the sky.

Strange secret compartments in their ever-growing torsos opened up, revealing giant rocket boosters and the latest in advanced aviation technology. Steel panels on their faces and bodies expanded wildly as their complex structures swelled to highly improbable proportions.

Suddenly, flames shot out of their retro-thrusters as their bodies rose into the air. In no time at all, two gigantic robots were flying in hot pursuit of the Amazing Captain Underpants.

"George and Harold are in BIG trouble now," said Melvin Sneedly, as he read Rule #7,734 of Mr. Krupp's official school rulebook out loud: *"It is against the rules for students to transform into giant flying robots during afternoon recess!"*

The *real* George and Harold, however, had more on their minds at that moment than a few broken rules. They watched the action unfold on a big-screen television that Wedgie Woman's horrible hair had built by combining the spare parts of a fish tank and an electric toothbrush.

The colossal robots surrounded Captain Underpants, but surprisingly, the Waistband Warrior looked happy to see them.

"George! Harold!" said Captain Underpants. "My, how you boys have grown! And I didn't know you could fly. That's great! Now you can help me fight for Truth, Justice, and all that is Pre-Shrunk and Cottony!"

But the gigantic robots didn't respond. Instead, they hovered close to Captain Underpants as their steel chest plates opened up. Suddenly, two extendable robotic arms reached out and began showering Captain Underpants with liquid spray starch.

"What-what are you doing?" cried Captain Underpants. "That's *SPRAY STARCH*! It's the only thing in the world that can take away my super powers!!!"

The Waistband Warrior screamed in
horror as he began falling through the
sky. Robo-George quickly swooped down,
grabbed the helpless hero, and hung him by
his waistband on a tall pole high above the
city streets.

# CHAPTER 20
# YOU AXED FOR IT

"Hooray!" cried Wedgie Woman as she turned off her new TV. "My plan worked. Now it's time to take over the world!"

"But what about us?" asked Harold.

"Don't worry," said Wedgie Woman. "I've got a big surprise for you two." She took a heavy battle-axe and tied it up with a rope. Then she leaned the axe toward George and Harold, and lit a candle under the rope.

"When the flame burns through the rope," said Wedgie Woman, "all your problems will be over. Get the point?"

"Not really," said George.

"Don't worry," laughed Wedgie Woman. "You will soon enough."

Wedgie Woman laughed a horrible laugh. Then she dashed out the door to take on the world!

George and Harold watched as the flame began burning through the rope. They cringed as the impending doom of the axe blade came closer and closer.

"Well," said George, "it looks like this is the end."

"Maybe not," said Harold. "Maybe the blade will fall and slice through our ropes and not harm us at all."

"I doubt it," said George. "That kind of thing only happens in really lame adventure stories."

Suddenly, the blade fell and sliced through the ropes, not harming George or Harold at all. The two boys looked at each other and decided it was best not to comment on the situation.

Thok

# CHAPTER 21

# THE WOOTHLESS WEVENGE OF THE WICKED WEDGIE WOMAN

Wedgie Woman headed to the center of town to meet up with Robo-George and the Harold 2000. "Well done, my precious robots," said Wedgie Woman affectionately.

"What's all this then?" said a policeman who had just arrived on the scene.

"Er-nothing, officer," said Wedgie Woman. "Just the beginning of my TOTAL WORLD DOMINATION!"

"Oh, O.K.," said the cop. "Hey, *wait a minute*!" But before the police officer could voice his objections, a twisted dreadlock from Wedgie Woman's head shot out and grabbed the cop by the back of his underwear.

The colossal Harold 2000 lifted the officer and hung him from a stop sign.

"Owie, *WOWIE*!" cried the cop.

Soon more police officers headed to the scene, but they all met with the same terrible fate as the first policeman.

Before long, every cop in the city was hanging from a street sign.

"Call the National Guard!" screamed the Chief of Police. "Call the Army—call the Marines—call a *HAIRSTYLIST*!"

Soon, the armed forces arrived with a whole fleet of tanks and helicopters. But everybody was afraid to shoot. Wedgie Woman was just too quick.

The giant robots stomped around the city as Wedgie Woman barked out her commands. "Everybody on Earth must obey ME!" cried the Wicked Wedgie Woman. "If anybody refuses, they'll get the WEDGE! If anybody tries to stop me, it's WEDGIE TIME! Bow down to me . . . or *WELCOME TO WEDGIEVILLE!*"

Soon George and Harold arrived at the scene. They hid in some bushes and watched the terror unfold.

"We've got to rescue Captain Underpants," whispered George. "He's the only one who can save the world!"

"But how?" whispered Harold. "He's got no super powers left!"

"Sure he does!" said George. "Starch doesn't really take away super powers . . . he just *THINKS* it does. We've got to change his mind!"

"I sure hope we can!" said Harold.

# CHAPTER 22
# THEY CAN'T

George and Harold ran to the pole where the heartbroken hero was hanging.

"Hey, Captain Underpants," cried Harold. "You've got to come down from there and save the city!"

"C-can't," whined the Waistband Warrior. "N-need fabric softener!"

"No you *don't* need fabric softener!" said George sternly. "That was just a dumb joke in one of our comics!"

"But you don't understand," said Captain Underpants. "Starch is the enemy of under-wear. Only fabric softener can save me!"

*"RATS!"* said Harold in frustration. "Hey, George, are there any stores around here?"

"Yeah," said George. "A new one just opened down on Oak Street."

"Then let's go buy some fabric softener," said Harold. "It'll be easier than trying to reason with the guy."

"How's that going to help?" asked George.

"It's all in his mind," Harold explained. "If he *believes* that fabric softener will save him, then it probably will. I think it's called 'the Placenta Effect.'"

So George and Harold ran to Oak Street. "What's the name of that store?" asked Harold.

"I can't remember," said George. "I think it's called 'Everything Except . . . umm—'"

"Aww, *maaaan*!" said George.

*"We're doomed!"* cried Harold.

"Listen," said George. "We've got to make another comic book!"

"Now?!!?" asked Harold.

"It's our only hope," said George. "The fate of the entire planet is in our hands!"

So the two boys bought some paper and a few pencils, and got down to work.

Twenty-two minutes later, George and Harold had created an all-new Captain Underpants adventure. They ran back to the pole where Captain Underpants was hanging and tossed their new comic up to him.

"This is no time to be reading comics," said Captain Underpants.

"Just read it, bub!" said Harold.

"Yeah," said George. "You might learn something!"

## CHAPTER 24
# THE PLACENTA EFFECT

"Wow," said Captain Underpants. "I didn't realize that I had the power within me all along to overcome the evils of starch."

"JUST SAY THE WORDS!" shouted George and Harold.

"O.K.," said Captain Underpants. "But I think it's a great metaphor for—"

"JUST SAY THE WORDS!" yelled George and Harold.

"*Alright!*" said Captain Underpants. "But all I'm saying is that—"

"*JUST SAY THE WORDS!*" screamed George and Harold.

"You know," said Captain Underpants, "you kids have *NO* feel for dramatic tension!" Then he cleared his throat and spoke in a powerful voice. "I SUMMON THE POWER OF UNDERPANTYWORLD!"

Suddenly, Captain Underpants rose triumphantly into the air. He was free at last!

When the gigantic robots saw that Captain Underpants had escaped, the Harold 2000 launched its rocket arms at our hero.

Captain Underpants grabbed the giant robo-arms and swung them around toward his foes.

"These might come in handy," said the Waistband Warrior.

# CHAPTER 25

# THE INCREDIBLY GRAPHIC VIOLENCE CHAPTER (IN FLIP-O-RAMA™)

## WARNING:

The following chapter contains scenes that are so violent and naughty, you aren't allowed to view them.

We're not kidding.

DO NOT READ
THE FOLLOWING CHAPTER!
Don't even look at it.
Just skip ahead to page 156,
and don't ask any questions.

P.S. Don't breathe on it, either.

# PILKEY® BRAND

# D-RAMA

## HERE'S HOW IT WORKS!

### STEP 1

First, give yourself eleven spankings and one time-out. Then, place your *left* hand inside the dotted lines marked "LEFT HAND HERE." Hold the book open *flat*.

### STEP 2

Grasp the *right-hand* page with your right thumb and index finger (inside the dotted lines marked "RIGHT THUMB HERE").

### STEP 3

Now *quickly* flip the right-hand page back and forth until the picture appears to be *animated*.

(For extra fun, try adding your own sound-effects!)

# FLIP-O-RAMA 1

(pages 141 and 143)

Remember, flip *only* page 141.
While you are flipping, be sure you
can see the picture on page 141
*and* the one on page 143.
If you flip quickly, the two
pictures will start to look like
<u>one</u> *animated* picture.

Don't forget to
add your own sound-effects!

**LEFT HAND HERE**

# ROUGHIN' UP
# THE ROBO-GEORGE

RIGHT
THUMB
HERE

# ROUGHIN' UP
# THE ROBO-GEORGE

# FLIP-O-RAMA 2

(pages 145 and 147)

Remember, flip *only* page 145.
While you are flipping, be sure you
can see the picture on page 145
*and* the one on page 147.
If you flip quickly, the two
pictures will start to look like
<u>one</u> *animated* picture.

Don't forget to
add your own sound-effects!

**LEFT HAND HERE**

# HORRIBLY HURTIN' THE HAROLD 2000

RIGHT
THUMB
HERE

# HORRIBLY HURTIN'
# THE HAROLD 2000

# FLIP-O-RAMA 3

(pages 149 and 151)

Remember, flip *only* page 149.
While you are flipping, be sure you
can see the picture on page 149
*and* the one on page 151.
If you flip quickly, the two
pictures will start to look like
<u>one</u> *animated* picture.

Don't forget to
add your own sound-effects!

**LEFT HAND HERE**

# LET'S PUT
# OUR HEADS
# TOGETHER

RIGHT
THUMB
HERE

# LET'S PUT
# OUR HEADS
# TOGETHER

# FLIP-O-RAMA 4

(pages 153 and 155)

Remember, flip *only* page 153.
While you are flipping, be sure you
can see the picture on page 153
*and* the one on page 155.
If you flip quickly, the two
pictures will start to look like
<u>one</u> *animated* picture.

Don't forget to
add your own sound-effects!

**LEFT HAND HERE**

# THE SUPER-SMASHY
# CYBER SLAM

RIGHT
THUMB
HERE

RIGHT
INDEX
FINGER
HERE

# THE SUPER-SMASHY
# CYBER SLAM

156

# CHAPTER 26
# REVERSE PSYCHOLOGY 2

The giant robots were defeated, but the battle was not over yet. Harold ran back to their tree house to grab the 3-D Hypno-Ring, while George ran back to Everything Except Fabric Softener for some more supplies.

Soon George returned to the center of town carrying a big cardboard box filled with spray cans.

"What are you doing with that?" asked Harold, who had just arrived with the 3-D Hypno-Ring.

"I'm taking this *Extra-Strength Spray Starch* someplace where Wedgie Woman won't be able to find it!" George shouted rather loudly.

*"Extra-Strength Spray Starch?"* cried the
Wicked Wedgie Woman. "That's just what I
need!" Her winding hair lashed out at
George, stopping him dead in his tracks.
Then nine twisting braids each grabbed a can
from the box and began spraying them at
Captain Underpants.

A huge cloud of mist filled the air, covering everything in sight, and making these two pages incredibly easy to draw.

When the cloud finally lifted, all of Wedgie Woman's hair was gone. In fact, all of EVERYBODY'S hair was gone.

"See?" George explained. "There was no spray starch in this box. This box was just a cleverly disguised carton of hair remover. I used *reverse psychology* on her."

"Aaugh!" screamed Harold, as he clutched his bald head. "My mom's gonna lay hard-boiled eggs when she sees me!"

"Relax," said George. "Our hair will grow back!"

"That's easy for you to say," said Harold. "Your hair was only half an inch long!"

# CHAPTER 27
# REVERSE REVERSE PSYCHOLOGY

"Well, Wedgie Woman," said Captain Underpants. "It's off to jail with you!"

"Wait a second," said Harold. "We'll take care of Wedgie Woman. You go back to the school, put some clothes on, then wash your face."

"Yeah, bub," said George. "Use plenty of water! We've got work to do."

"O.K.," said Captain Underpants.

So Captain Underpants did as he was told, and in no time at all he was back to his Kruppy old self. It was now time to transform Wedgie Woman back to her old self, too . . . *with some slight modifications.*

"O.K.," said Harold, "remember when we hypnotized Ms. Ribble, and she did the opposite of everything we wanted her to do?"

"Yeah," said George.

"Well, if we want to set things right," Harold continued, "we've got to hypnotize her into doing the *opposite* of the opposite of what we want."

"I'm way ahead of you," said George.

So the two boys once again hypnotized their teacher. Only this time, they used reverse *reverse* psychology on her.

"From now on," said George, "you will ALWAYS be known as Wedgie Woman."

"You WILL keep all your super powers, too," said Harold.

"You WILL NOT go back to teaching fourth grade," said George.

"You WILL remember everything that happened in the last two weeks," said Harold.

"You WILL NOT change our grades back to normal," said George.

"You WILL NOT become the nicest teacher in the history of Jerome Horwitz Elementary School," said Harold.

"And you WILL NOT bake fresh chocolate chip cookies for our class every day," said George.

*"George!"* said Harold sternly. "Stop goofing around!"

"I can't help it," said George. "You should never hypnotize anybody when you're hungry!"

"O.K., O.K.," said Harold. "Let's just snap our fingers and PRAY that this works."


*SNAP!*

# CHAPTER 28

# TO MAKE A LONG STORY SHORT

It did.

# CHAPTER 29

# BETTER LIVING THROUGH HYPNOSIS

The next day, Ms. Ribble entered the class-room looking a whole lot friendlier than usual.

"Boys and girls," said Ms. Ribble, "I have some good news for you."

"Hooray!" cried the children.

"It's time for English class," said Ms. Ribble.

"Aww, *maaaan*," moaned the children.

"Today," said Ms. Ribble, "I've asked George and Harold to lead the class."

"Hooray!" cried the children.

"They're going to teach us about creative writing . . ." said Ms. Ribble.

"Aww, *maaaan*," moaned the children.

". . . by showing us how to make our own comic books!" said Ms. Ribble.

"Hooray!" cried the children.

"While they're doing that," said Ms. Ribble, "I'm going to pass out something for you all to work on. . . ."

"Aww, *maaaan*," moaned the children.

". . . Homemade chocolate chip cookies!" said Ms. Ribble.

"Hooray!" cried the children.

"This is awesome," said Harold, "but do you think it was right for us to change her personality like we did?"

"Sure, why not?" said George. "She's happier. She'll probably live longer!"

"You're right," said Harold. "I guess hypnosis is a pretty cool thing sometimes."

Then again (as we all know) sometimes it isn't.

"OH, NO!" screamed Harold.
"Here we go again!" screamed George.

If you didn't follow the instructions
on page 137 and had to punish yourself,
please send a self-addressed,
stamped business-sized envelope to:

Your name
and address

Ouchies! I gave myself eleven spankings
and a time-out. Send me something fun!
c/o Scholastic Inc.
P. O. Box 711
New York, NY 10013-0711

We'll send you something fun.